Teen

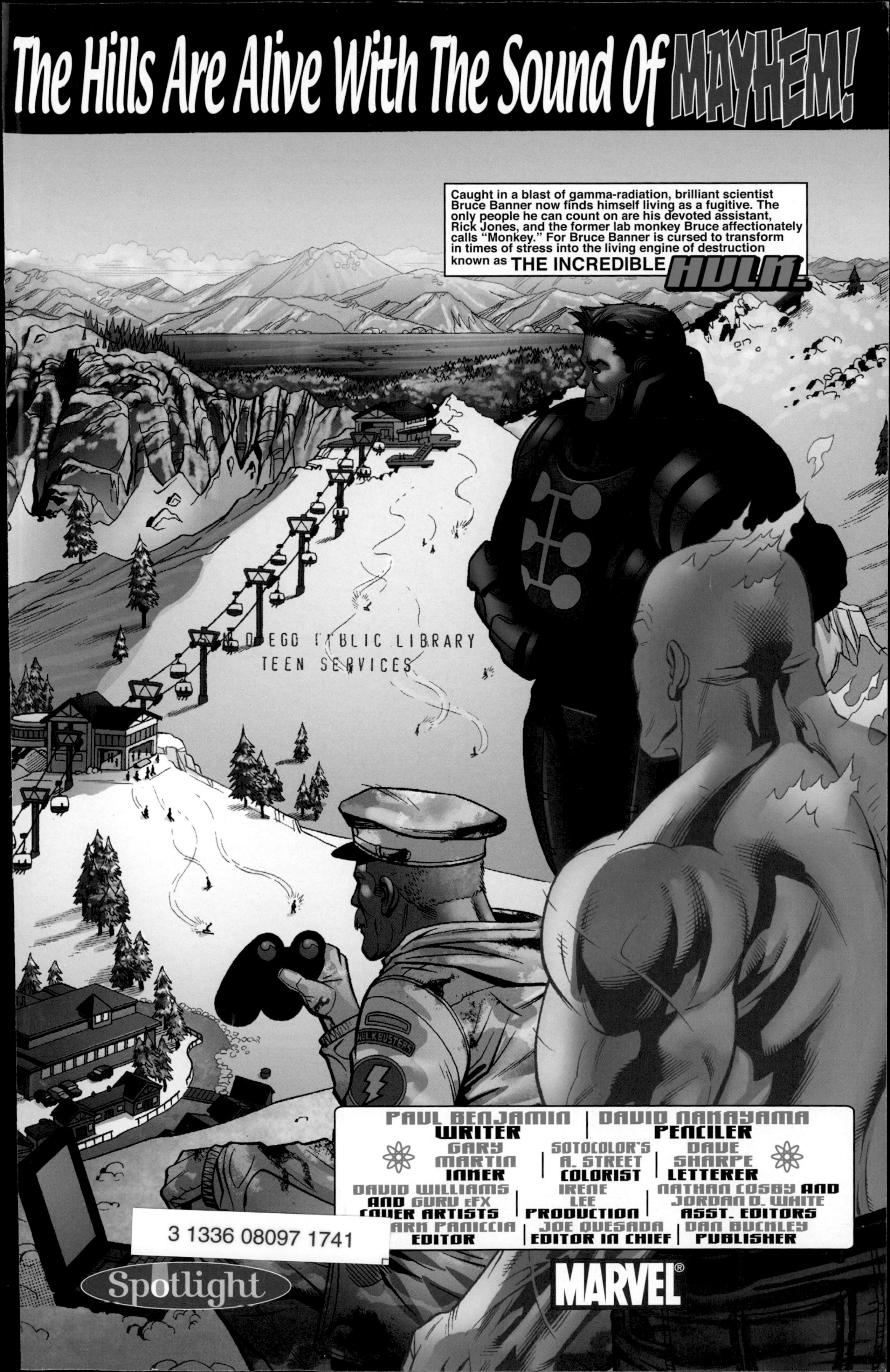
The Hills Are Alive With The Sound Of MAYHEM!
Caught in a blast of gamma-radiation, brilliant scientist Bruce Banner now finds himself living as a fugitive. The only people he can count on are his devoted assistant, Rick Jones, and the former lab monkey Bruce affectionately calls "Monkey." For Bruce Banner is cursed to transform in times of stress into the living engine of destruction known as THE INCREDIBLE HULK.
HULKBUSTERS
PAUL BENJAMIN WRITER
DAVID NAKAYAMA PENCILER
GARY MARTIN INKER
SOTOCOLOR'S A. STREET COLORIST
DAVE SHARPE LETTERER
DAVID WILLIAMS AND GURU eFX COVER ARTISTS
IRENE LEE PRODUCTION
NATHAN COSBY AND JORDAN D. WHITE ASST. EDITORS
ARK PANICCIA EDITOR
JOE QUESADA EDITOR IN CHIEF
DAN BUCKLEY PUBLISHER
Spotlight
MARVEL

VISIT US AT
www.abdopublishing.com

Reinforced library bound edition published in 2009 by Spotlight, a division of the ABDO Publishing Group, 8000 West 78th Street, Edina, Minnesota 55439. Spotlight produces high-quality reinforced library bound editions for schools and libraries. Published by agreement with Marvel Characters, Inc.

Library of Congress Cataloging-in-Publication Data

Benjamin, Paul, 1970-
  Mayhem! / Paul Benjamin, writer ; David Nakayama, penciler ; Gary Martin, inker ; Sotocolor's A. Street, colorist ; Dave Sharpe, letterer ; David Williams and GURU eFX , cover artists.
    p. cm. -- (Hulk)
  "Marvel."
  ISBN 978-1-59961-548-6 (reinforced lib. bound ed.)
  1. Graphic novels. [1. Graphic novels.] I. Nakayama, David, ill. II. Title.
  PZ7.7.B45May 2008
  [Fic]--dc22

                                                              2008000101

All Spotlight books have reinforced library bindings and are manufactured in the United States of America.

HIGH IN THE ROCKY MOUNTAINS, U.S.A.
Listen up, men. You're about to tackle the greatest threat to national security America has ever known.
HULKBUSTERS
The bombastic blowhard in the parka is General "Thunderbolt" Ross. He's been hunting me ever since my... accident.

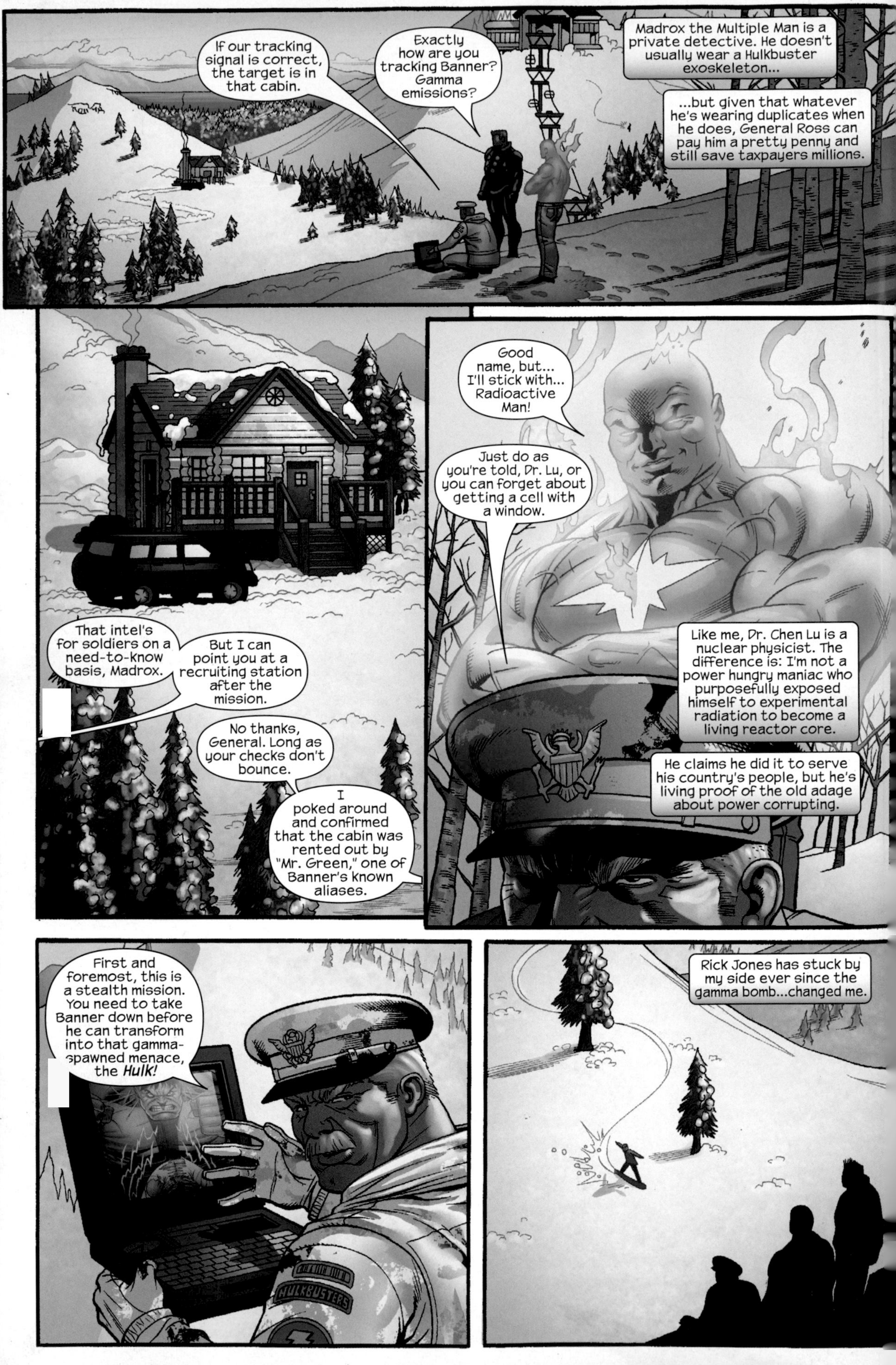

If our tracking signal is correct, the target is in that cabin.
Exactly how are you tracking Banner? Gamma emissions?
Madrox the Multiple Man is a private detective. He doesn't usually wear a Hulkbuster exoskeleton...
...but given that whatever he's wearing duplicates when he does, General Ross can pay him a pretty penny and still save taxpayers millions.
That intel's for soldiers on a need-to-know basis, Madrox.
But I can point you at a recruiting station after the mission.
No thanks, General. Long as your checks don't bounce.
I poked around and confirmed that the cabin was rented out by "Mr. Green," one of Banner's known aliases.
Good name, but... I'll stick with... Radioactive Man!
Just do as you're told, Dr. Lu, or you can forget about getting a cell with a window.
Like me, Dr. Chen Lu is a nuclear physicist. The difference is: I'm not a power hungry maniac who purposefully exposed himself to experimental radiation to become a living reactor core.
He claims he did it to serve his country's people, but he's living proof of the old adage about power corrupting.
First and foremost, this is a stealth mission. You need to take Banner down before he can transform into that gamma-spawned menace, the *Hulk!*
HULKBUSTERS
Rick Jones has stuck by my side ever since the gamma bomb...changed me.

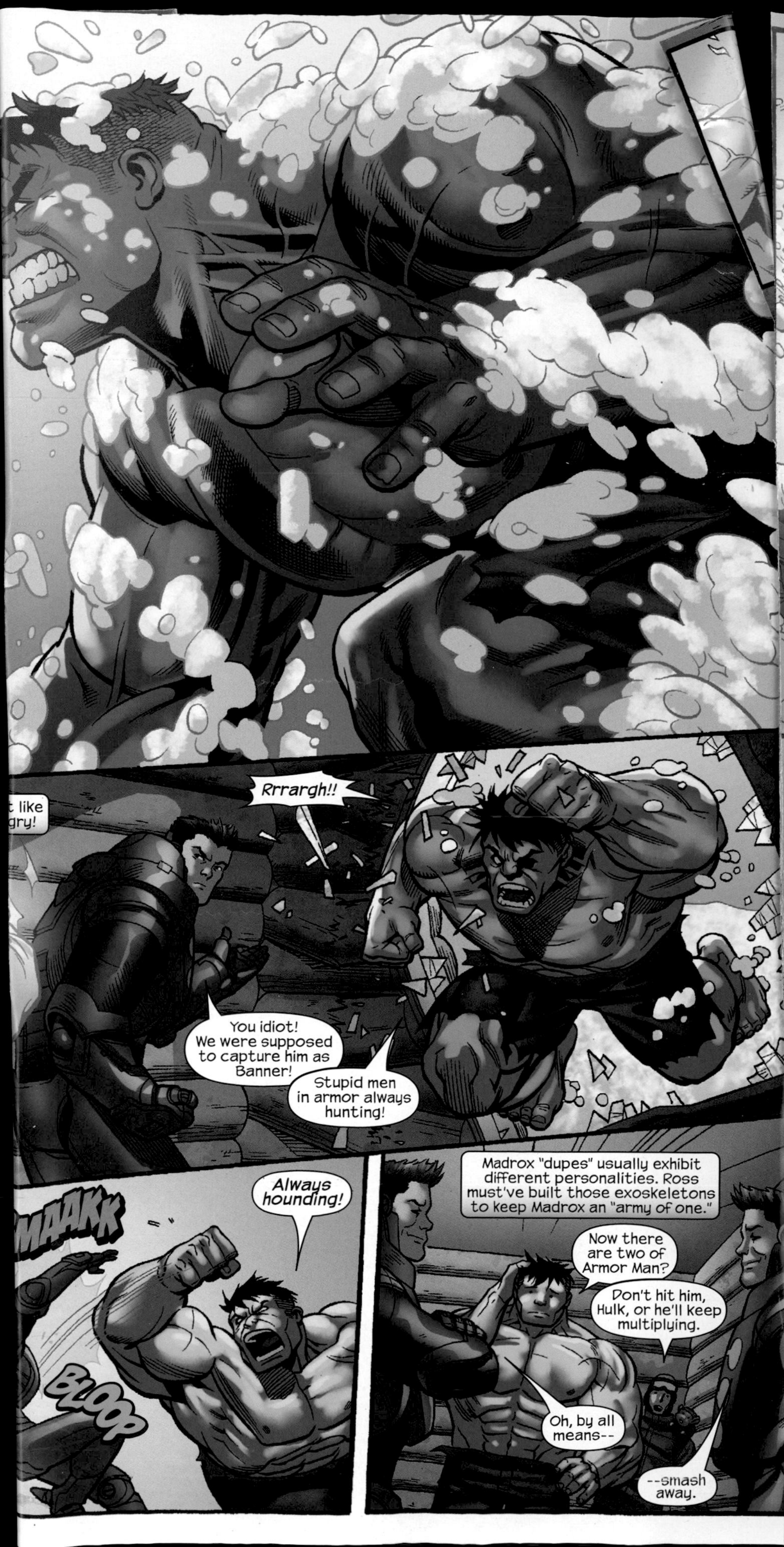
Rrrargh!!
You idiot! We were supposed to capture him as Banner!
Stupid men in armor always hunting!
Always hounding!
BLOOP
Madrox "dupes" usually exhibit different personalities. Ross must've built those exoskeletons to keep Madrox an "army of one."
Now there are two of Armor Man?
Don't hit him, Hulk, or he'll keep multiplying.
Oh, by all means--
--smash away.

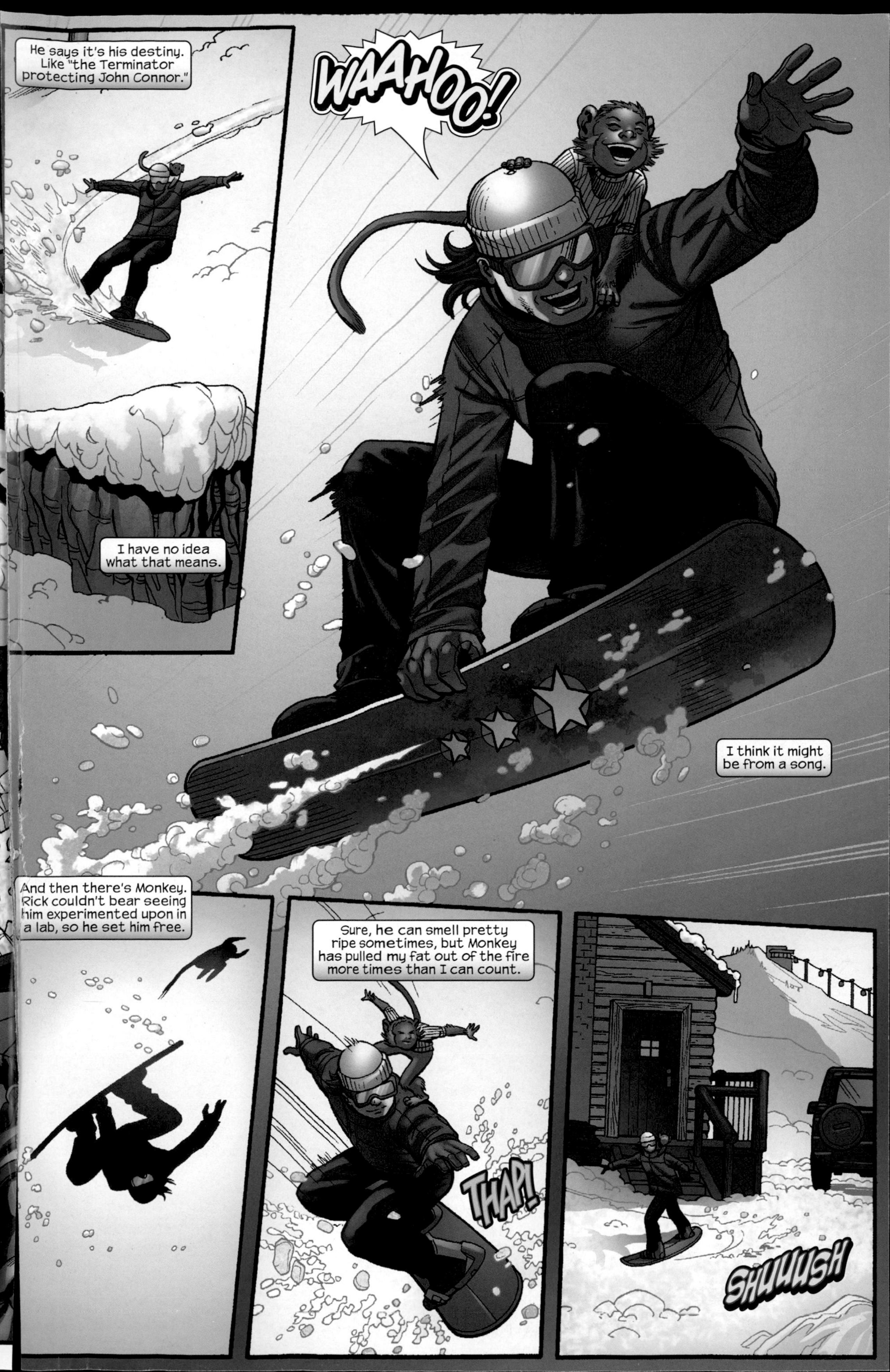
He says it's his destiny. Like "the Terminator protecting John Connor."
I have no idea what that means.
WAAHOO!
I think it might be from a song.
And then there's Monkey. Rick couldn't bear seeing him experimented upon in a lab, so he set him free.
Sure, he can smell pretty ripe sometimes, but Monkey has pulled my fat out of the fire more times than I can count.
THAP!
SHUUUSH

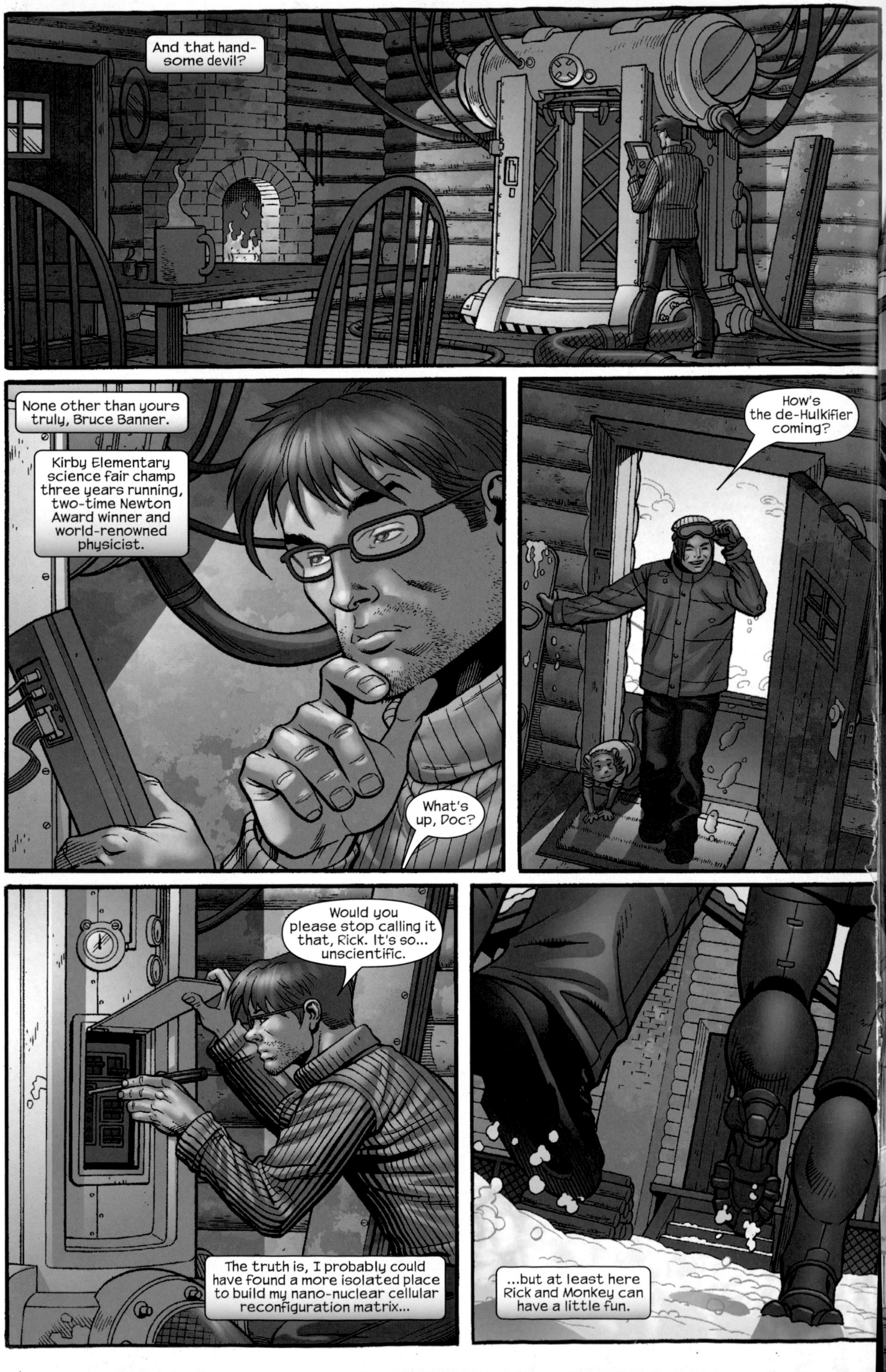
And that hand-some devil?
None other than yours truly, Bruce Banner.
Kirby Elementary science fair champ three years running, two-time Newton Award winner and world-renowned physicist.
What's up, Doc?
How's the de-Hulkifier coming?
Would you please stop calling it that, Rick. It's so... unscientific.
The truth is, I probably could have found a more isolated place to build my nano-nuclear cellular reconfiguration matrix...
...but at least here Rick and Monkey can have a little fun.

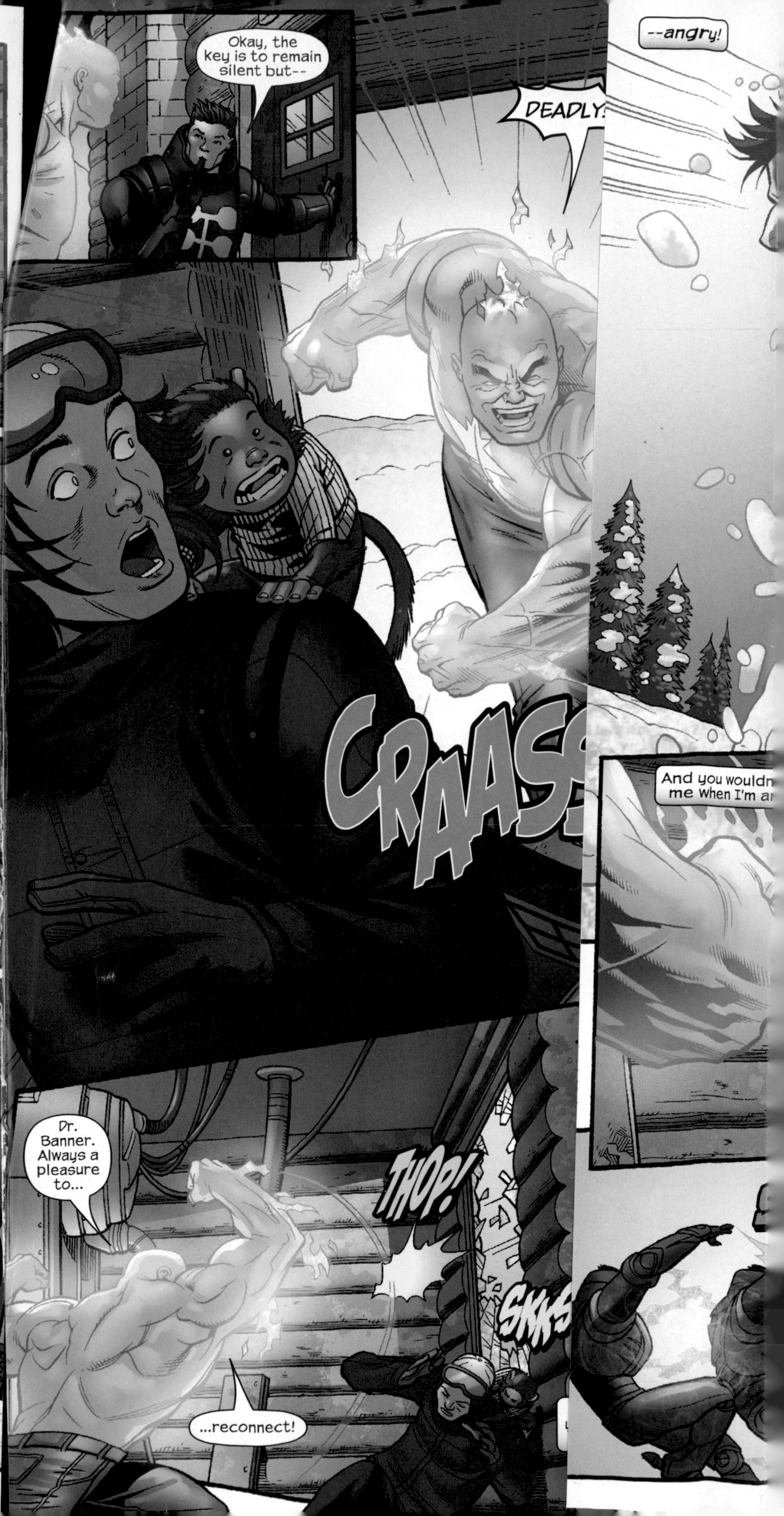
Okay, the key is to remain silent but--
DEADLY!
--angry!
CRAASS
Dr. Banner. Always a pleasure to...
THOP!
...reconnect!

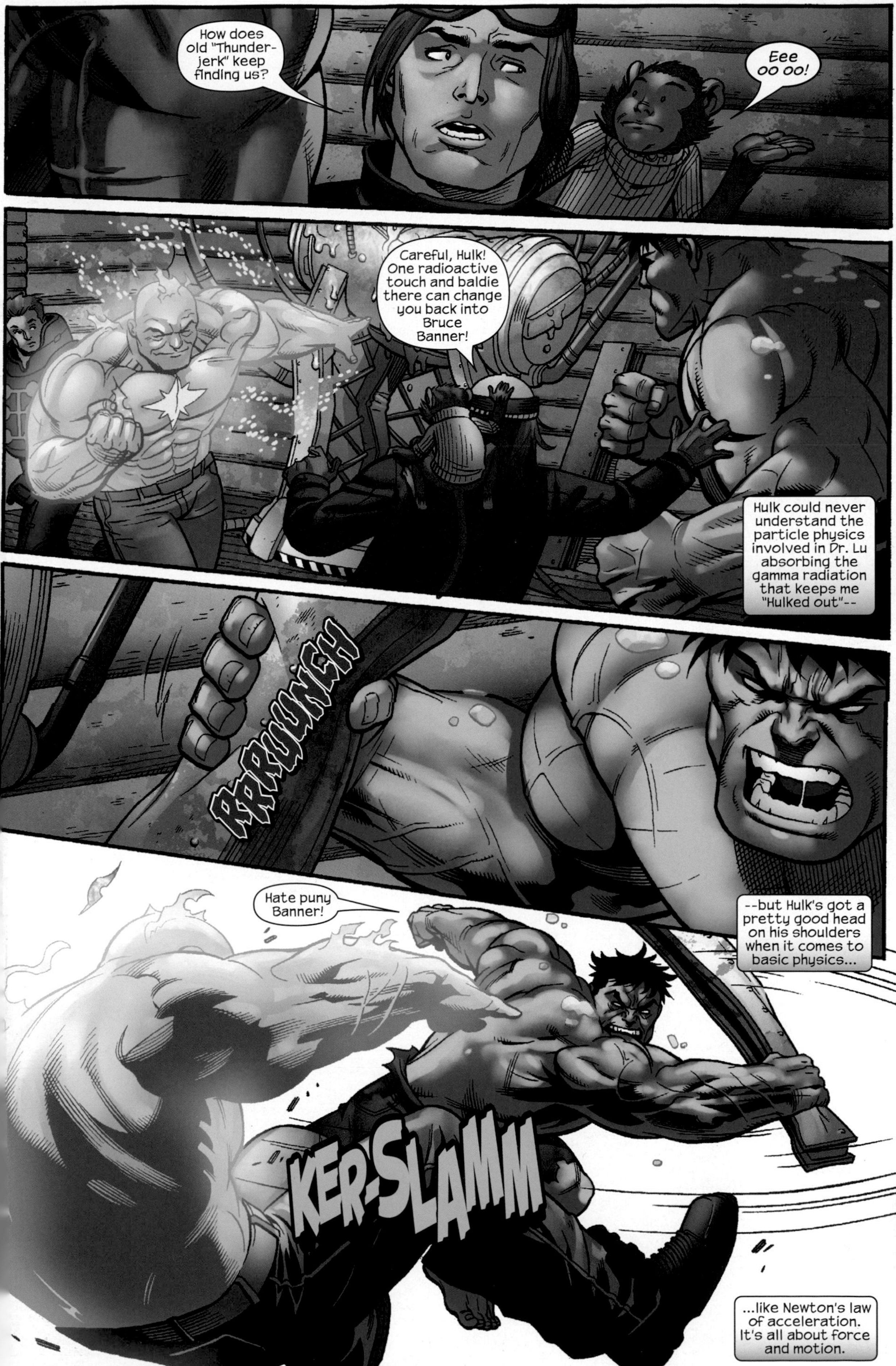
How does old "Thunder-jerk" keep finding us?
Eee oo oo!
Careful, Hulk! One radioactive touch and baldie there can change you back into Bruce Banner!
Hulk could never understand the particle physics involved in Dr. Lu absorbing the gamma radiation that keeps me "Hulked out"--
RRRUUNCH
Hate puny Banner!
--but Hulk's got a pretty good head on his shoulders when it comes to basic physics...
KER-SLAMM
...like Newton's law of acceleration. It's all about force and motion.

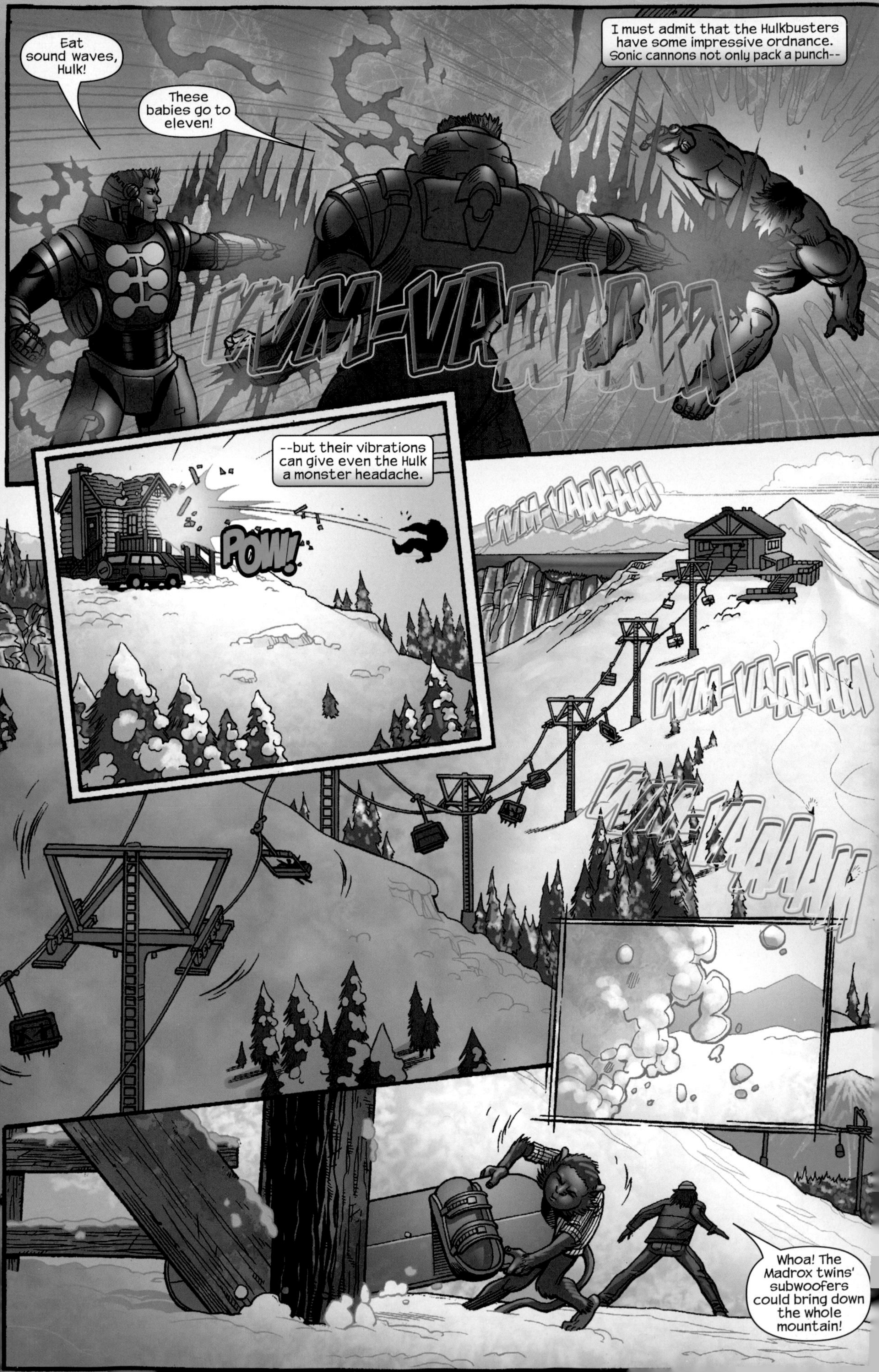
Eat sound waves, Hulk!
These babies go to eleven!
I must admit that the Hulkbusters have some impressive ordnance. Sonic cannons not only pack a punch--
VVM-VAAAAM
--but their vibrations can give even the Hulk a monster headache.
POW!
VVM-VAAAAM
VVM-VAAAAM
VVM-VAAAAM
Whoa! The Madrox twins' subwoofers could bring down the whole mountain!

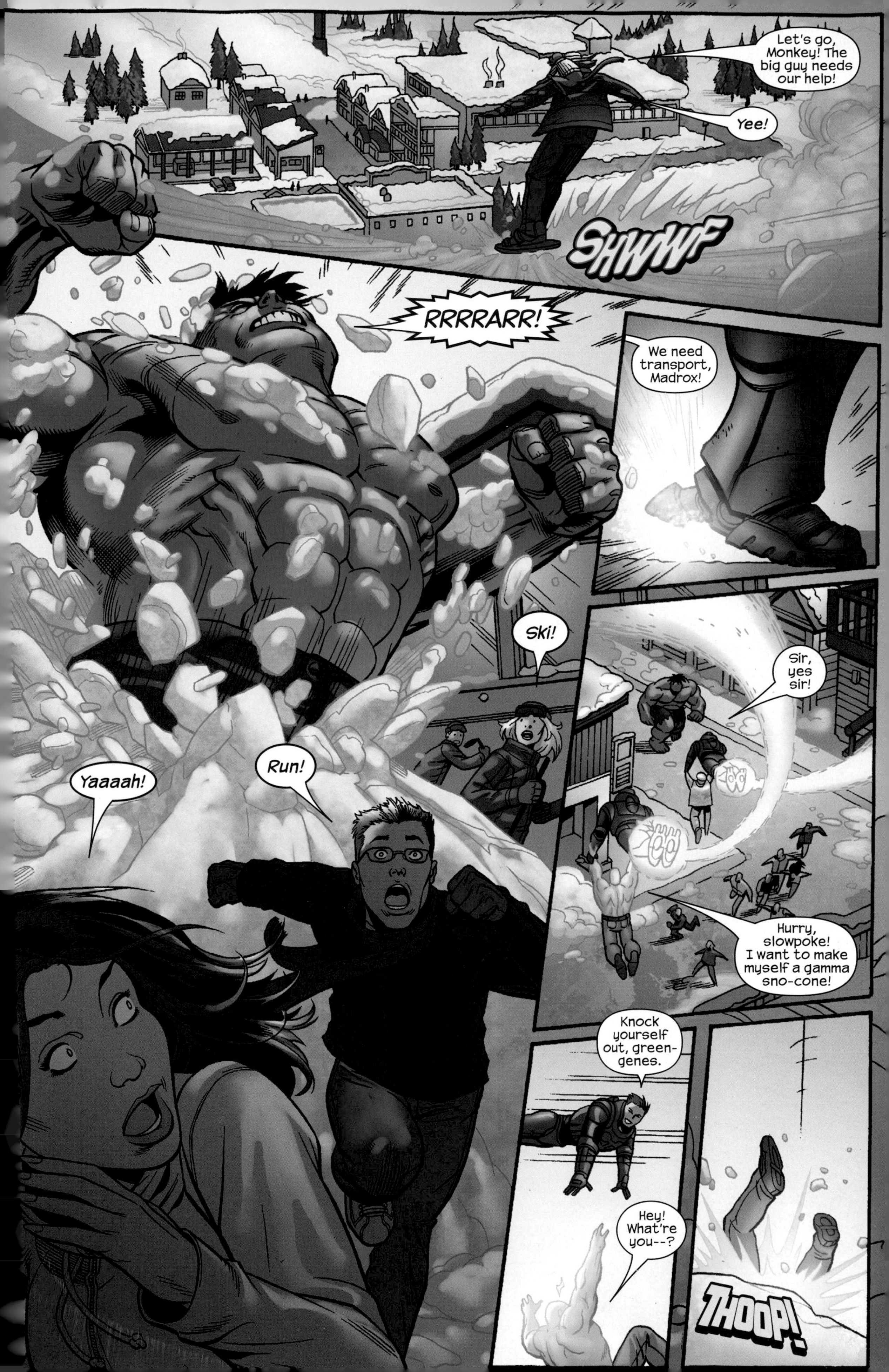
Let's go, Monkey! The big guy needs our help!
Yee!
SHWWF
RRRRARR!
We need transport, Madrox!
Ski!
Run!
Yaaaah!
Sir, yes sir!
Hurry, slowpoke! I want to make myself a gamma sno-cone!
Knock yourself out, green-genes.
Hey! What're you--?
THOOP!

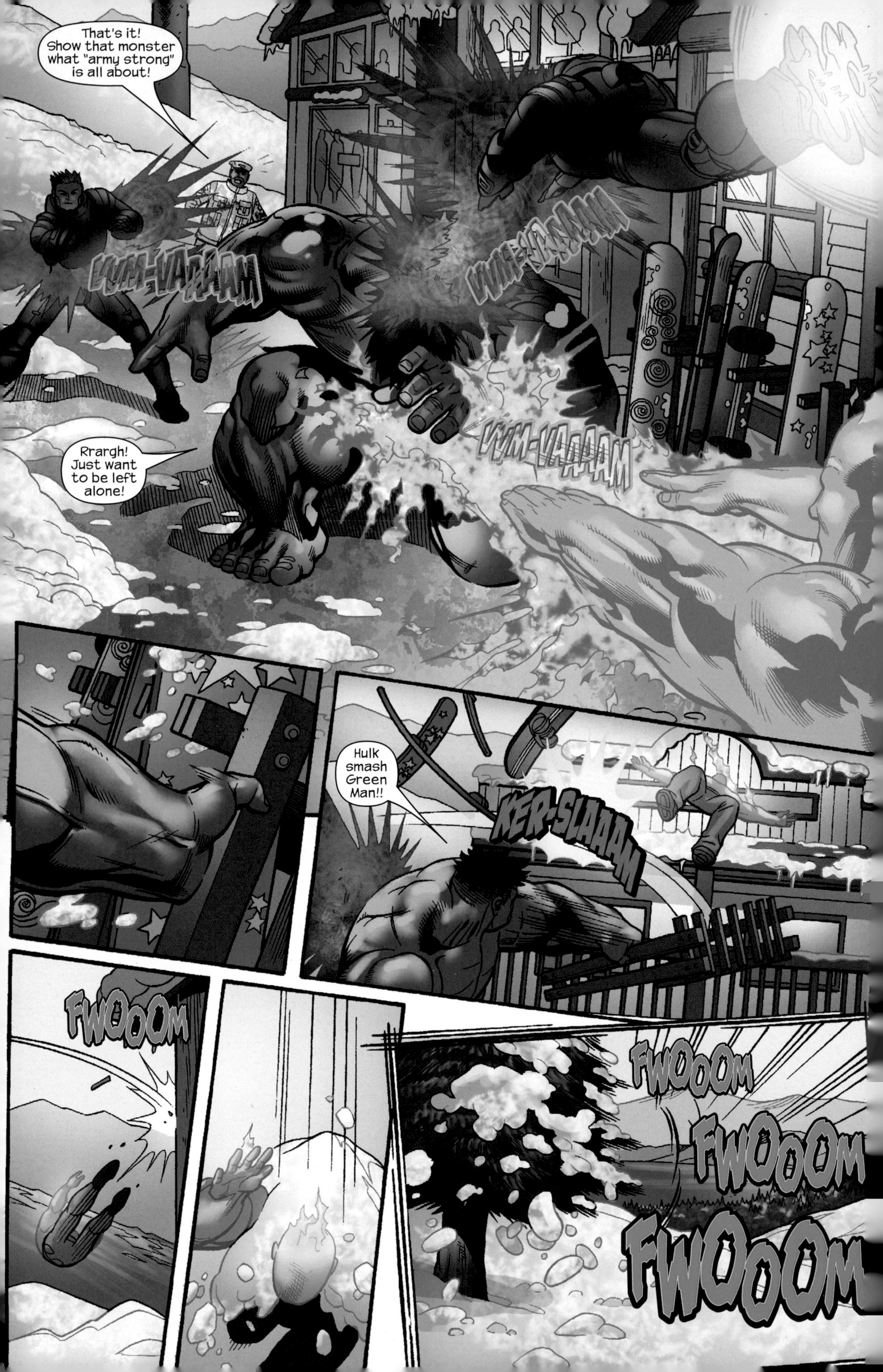
That's it! Show that monster what "army strong" is all about!
VVM-VAAAAM
VVM-VAAAAM
Rrargh! Just want to be left alone!
VVM-VAAAAM
Hulk smash Green Man!!
KER-SLAAAM
FWOOOM
FWOOOM
FWOOOM
FWOOOM

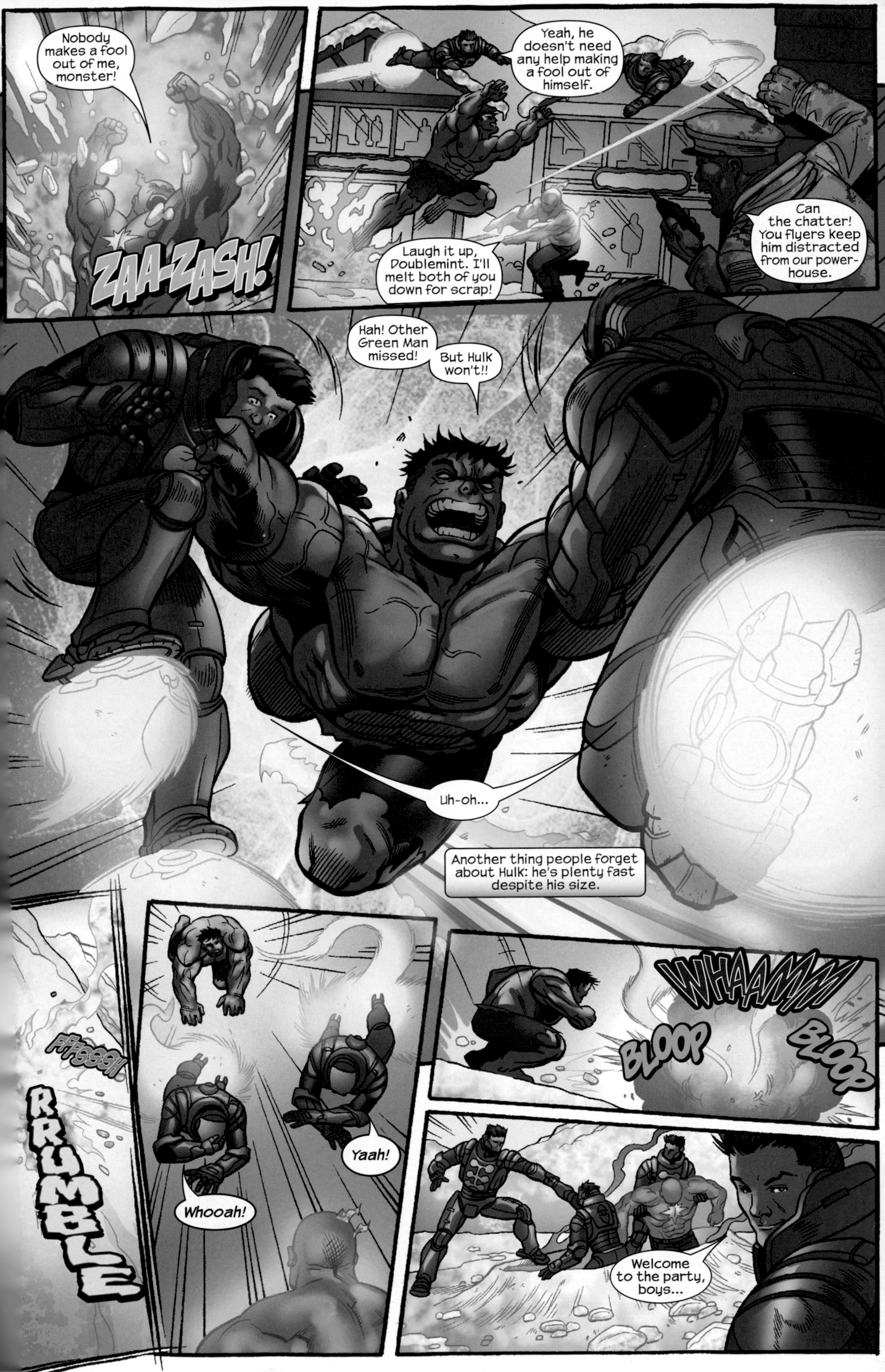
Nobody makes a fool out of me, monster!
ZAA-ZASH!
Yeah, he doesn't need any help making a fool out of himself.
Laugh it up, Doublemint. I'll melt both of you down for scrap!
Can the chatter! You flyers keep him distracted from our power-house.
Hah! Other Green Man missed!
But Hulk won't!!
Uh-oh...
Another thing people forget about Hulk: he's plenty fast despite his size.
FFSSSH
RRUMBLE
Yaah!
Whooah!
WHAAMM
BLOOP
BLOOP
Welcome to the party, boys...

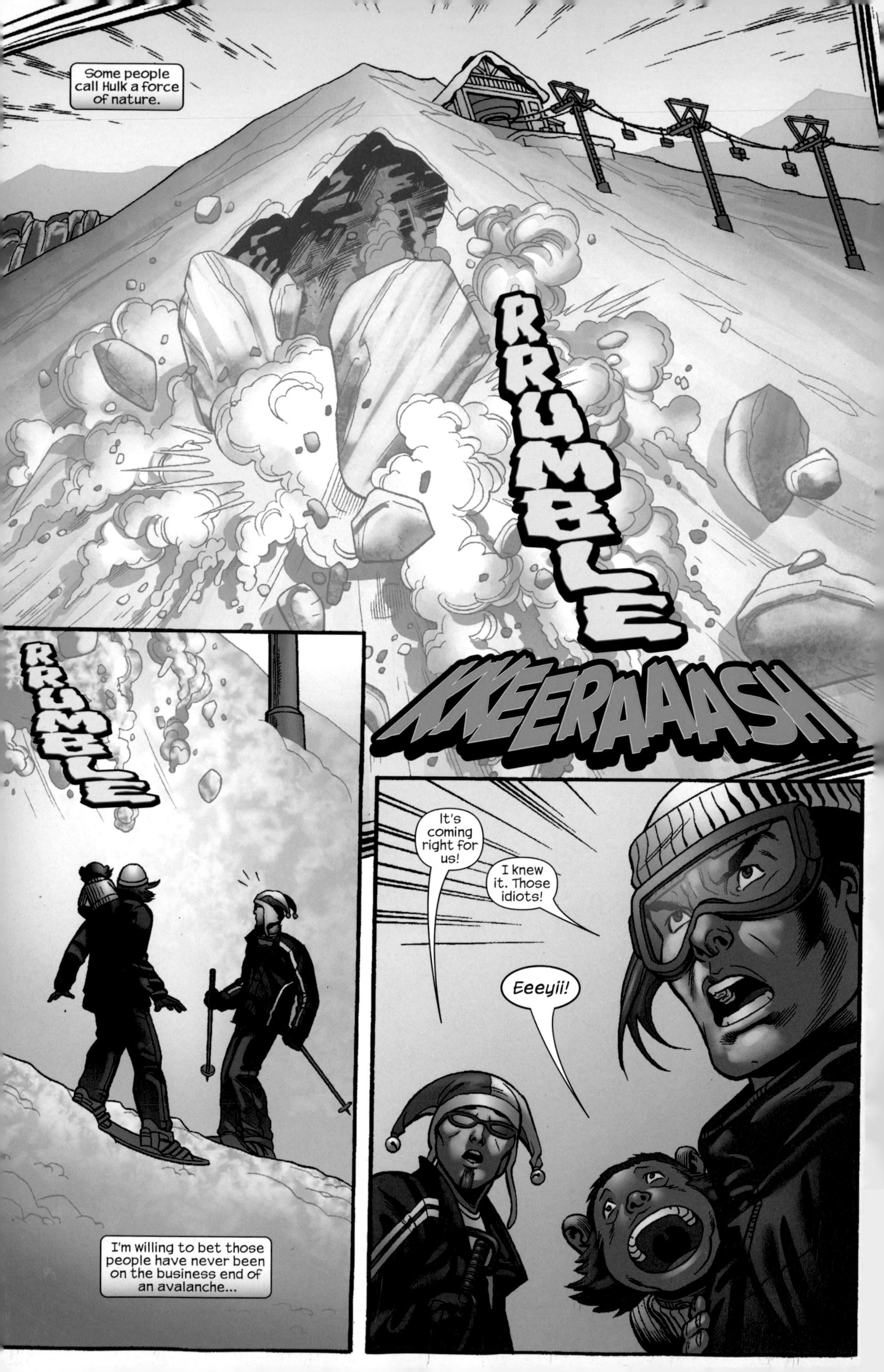
Some people call Hulk a force of nature.
RRUMBLE
KKEERAAASH
RRUMBLE
I'm willing to bet those people have never been on the business end of an avalanche...
It's coming right for us!
I knew it. Those idiots!
Eeeyii!

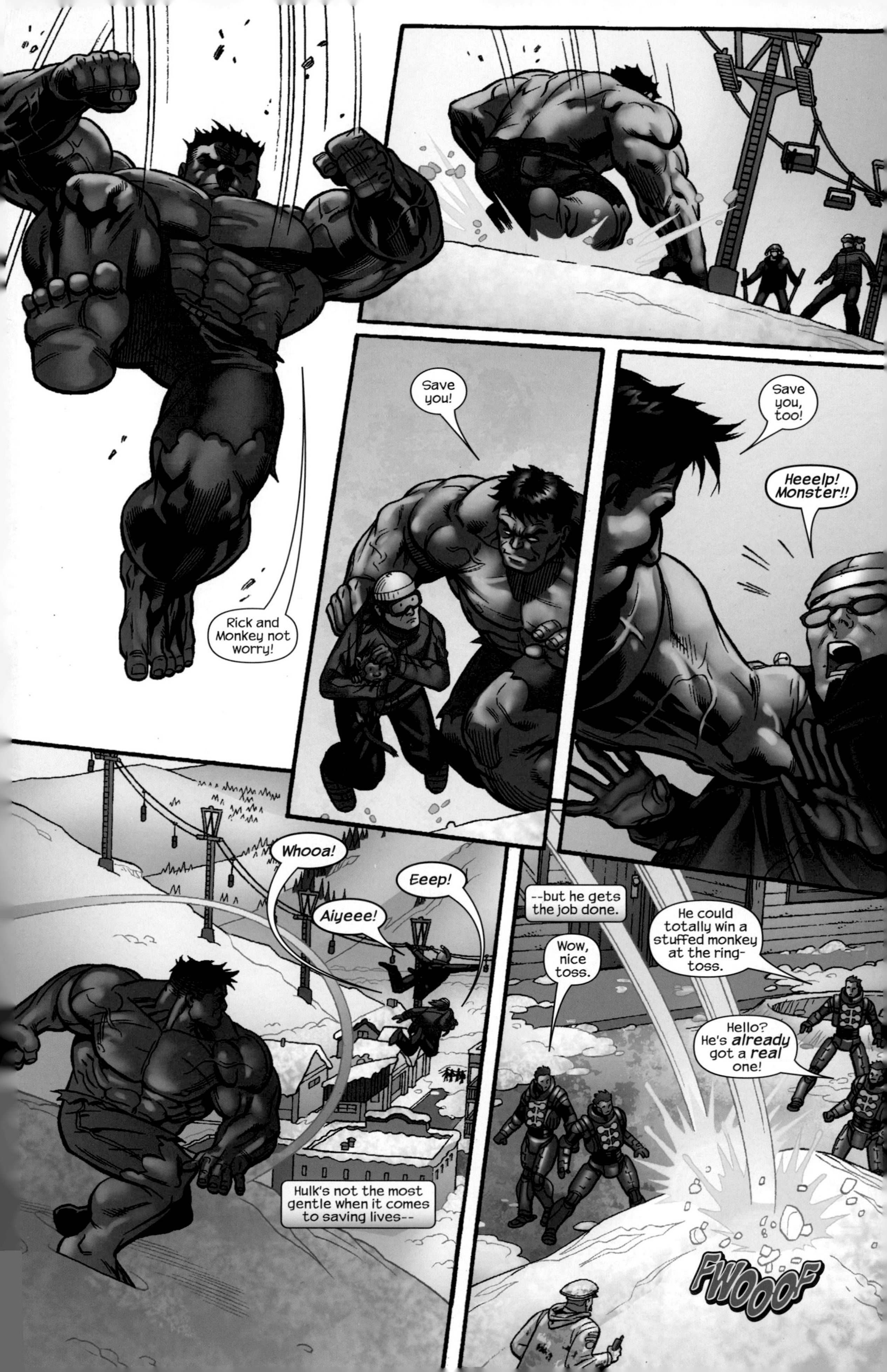
Rick and Monkey not worry!
Save you!
Save you, too!
Heeelp! Monster!!
Whooa!
Eeep!
Aiyeee!
Hulk's not the most gentle when it comes to saving lives--
--but he gets the job done.
Wow, nice toss.
He could totally win a stuffed monkey at the ring-toss.
Hello? He's already got a real one!
FWOOOF

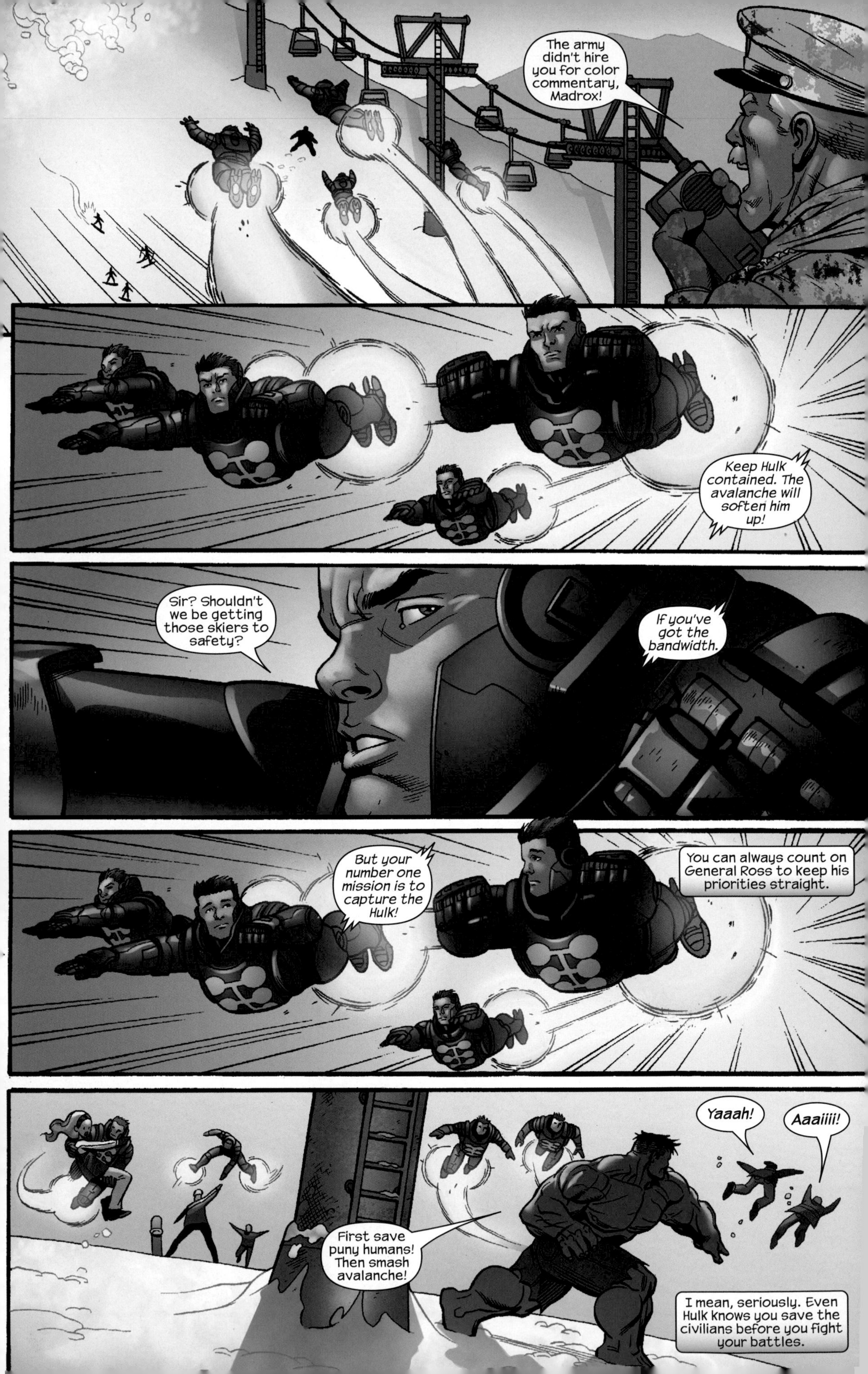
The army didn't hire you for color commentary, Madrox!
Keep Hulk contained. The avalanche will soften him up!
Sir? Shouldn't we be getting those skiers to safety?
If you've got the bandwidth.
But your number one mission is to capture the Hulk!
You can always count on General Ross to keep his priorities straight.
Yaaah!
Aaaiiii!
First save puny humans! Then smash avalanche!
I mean, seriously. Even Hulk knows you save the civilians before you fight your battles.

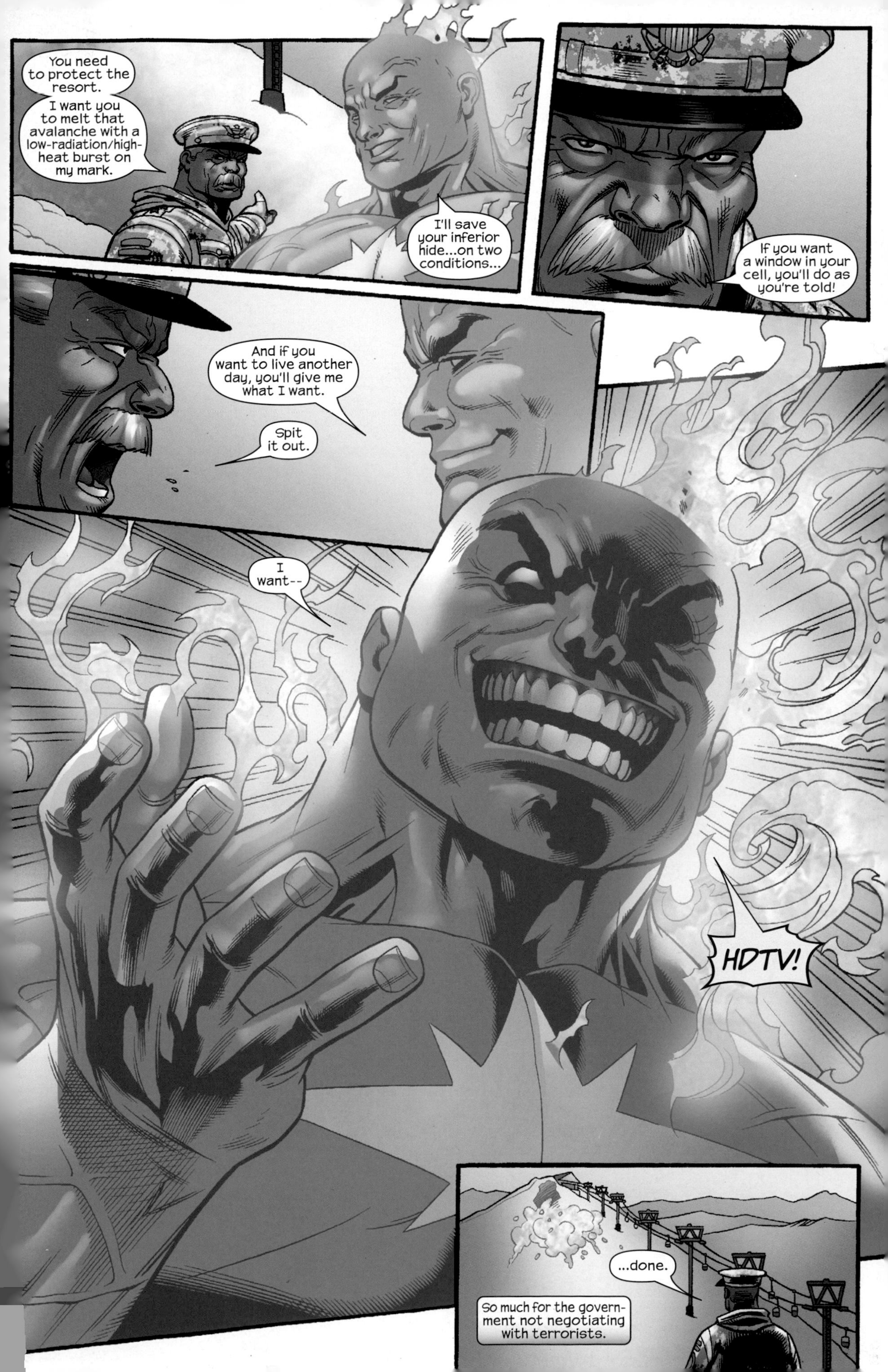
You need to protect the resort.
I want you to melt that avalanche with a low-radiation/high-heat burst on my mark.
I'll save your inferior hide...on two conditions...
If you want a window in your cell, you'll do as you're told!
And if you want to live another day, you'll give me what I want.
Spit it out.
I want--
HDTV!
...done.
So much for the government not negotiating with terrorists.

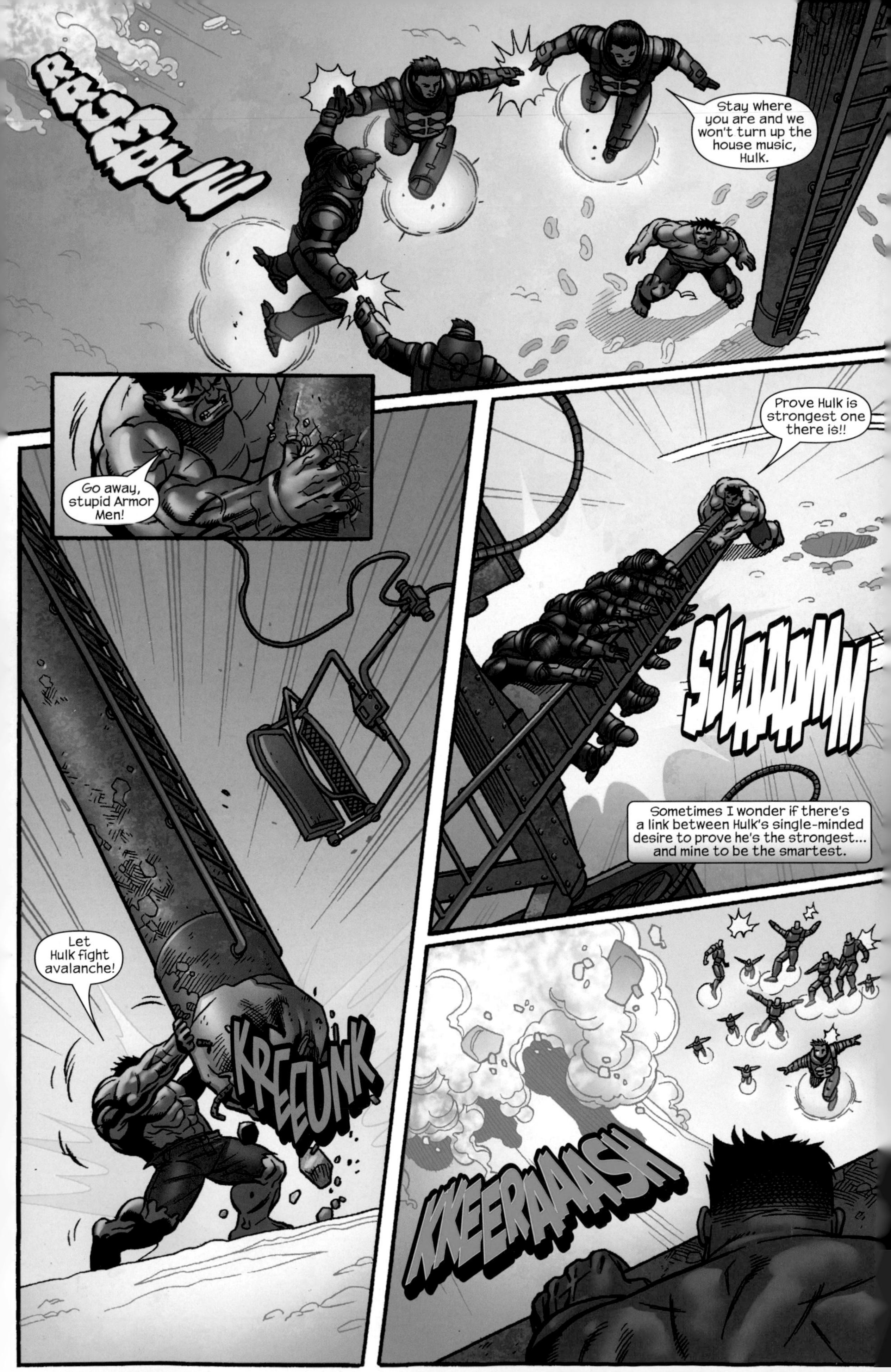
RRUMBLE
Stay where you are and we won't turn up the house music, Hulk.
Go away, stupid Armor Men!
Prove Hulk is strongest one there is!!
SLLAAAMM
Sometimes I wonder if there's a link between Hulk's single-minded desire to prove he's the strongest... and mine to be the smartest.
Let Hulk fight avalanche!
KREEUNK
KKEERAAASH

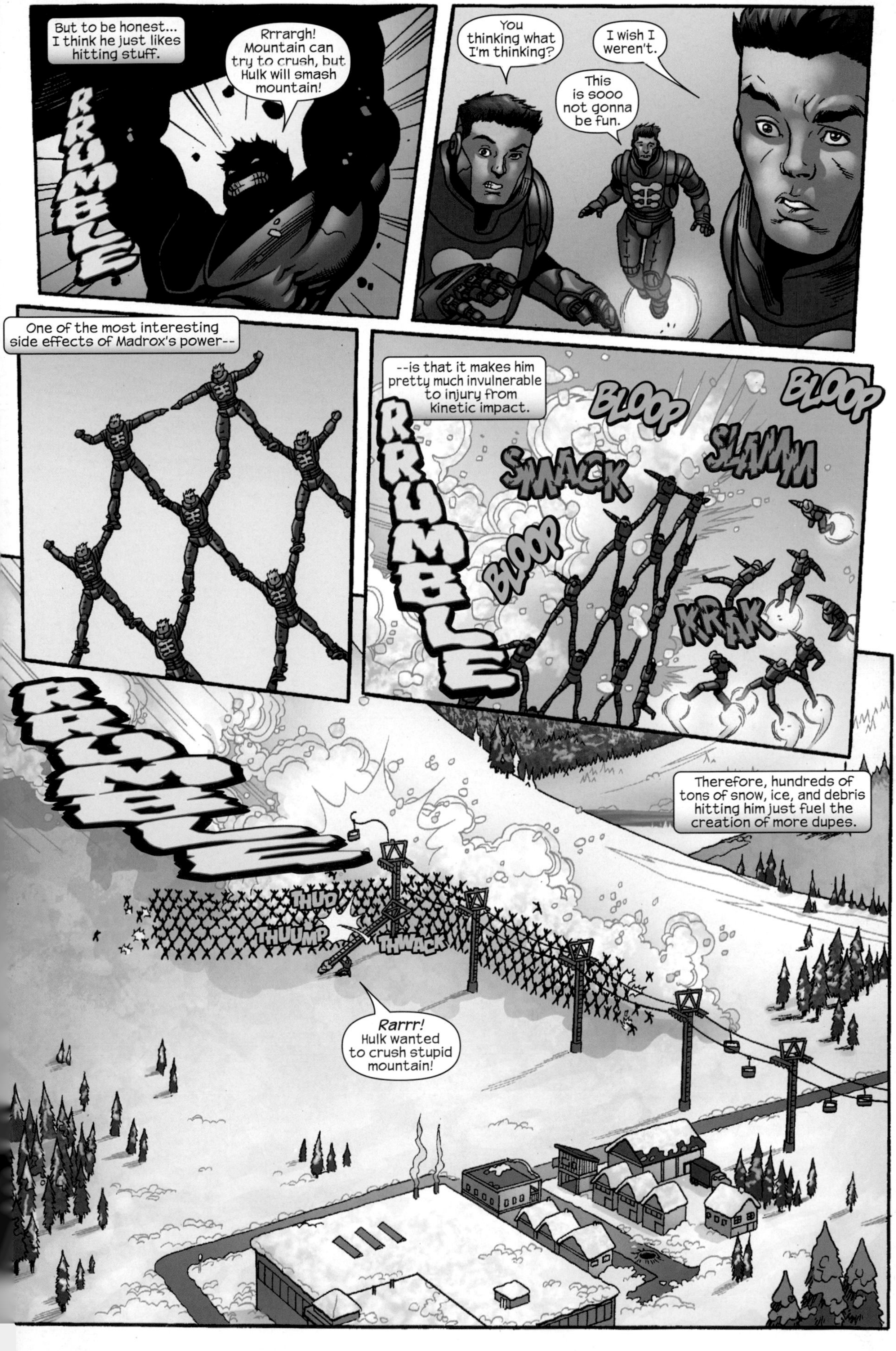
But to be honest... I think he just likes hitting stuff.
Rrrargh! Mountain can try to crush, but Hulk will smash mountain!
RRUMBLE
You thinking what I'm thinking?
I wish I weren't.
This is sooo not gonna be fun.
One of the most interesting side effects of Madrox's power--
--is that it makes him pretty much invulnerable to injury from kinetic impact.
RRUMBLE
BLOOP
BLOOP
SMACK
SLAMM
BLOOP
KRAK
RRUMBLE
THUD
THUUMP
THWACK
Therefore, hundreds of tons of snow, ice, and debris hitting him just fuel the creation of more dupes.
Rarrr! Hulk wanted to crush stupid mountain!

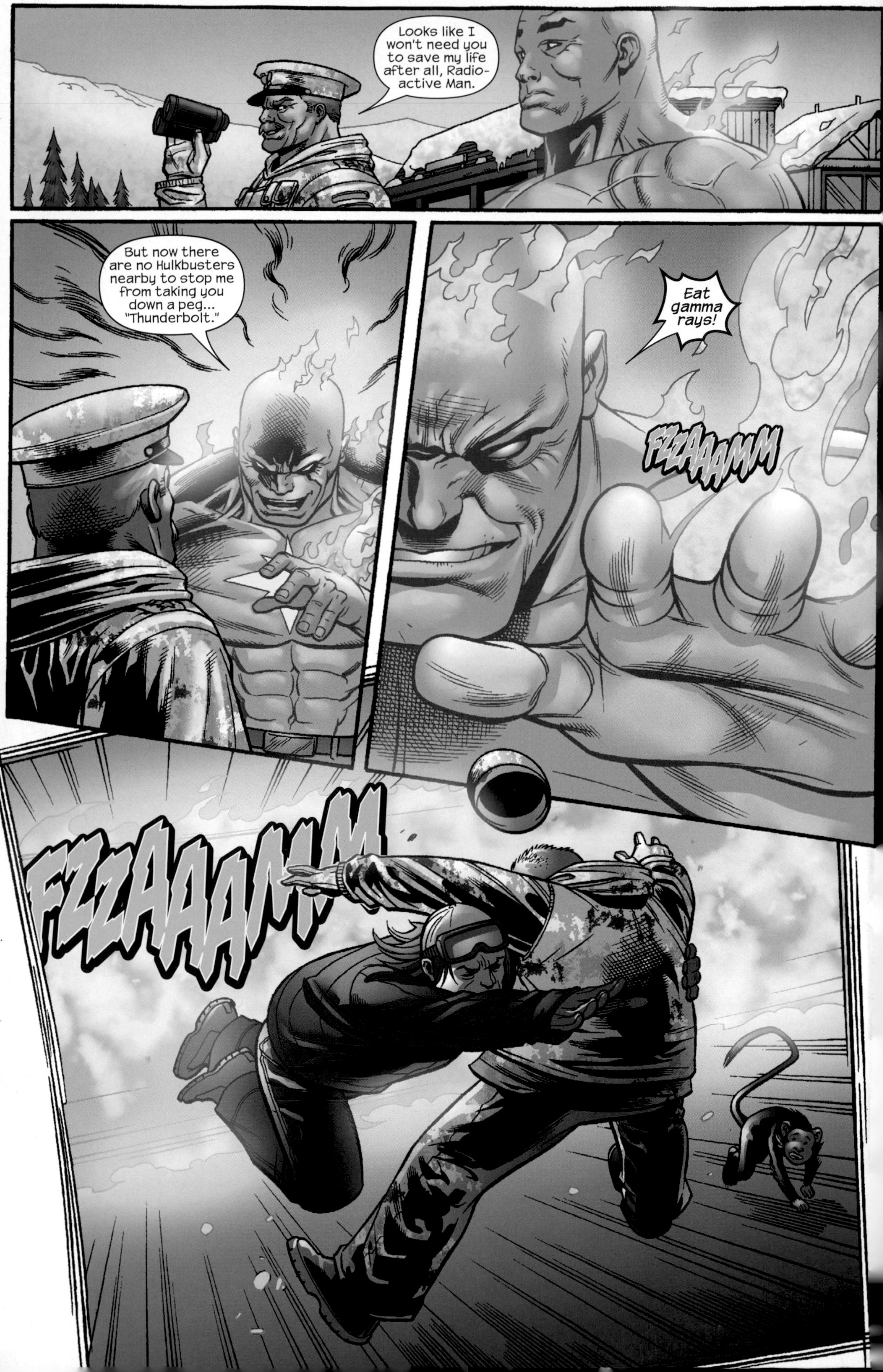
Looks like I won't need you to save my life after all, Radio-active Man.
But now there are no Hulkbusters nearby to stop me from taking you down a peg... "Thunderbolt."
Eat gamma rays!
FZZAAAMM
FZZAAAMM

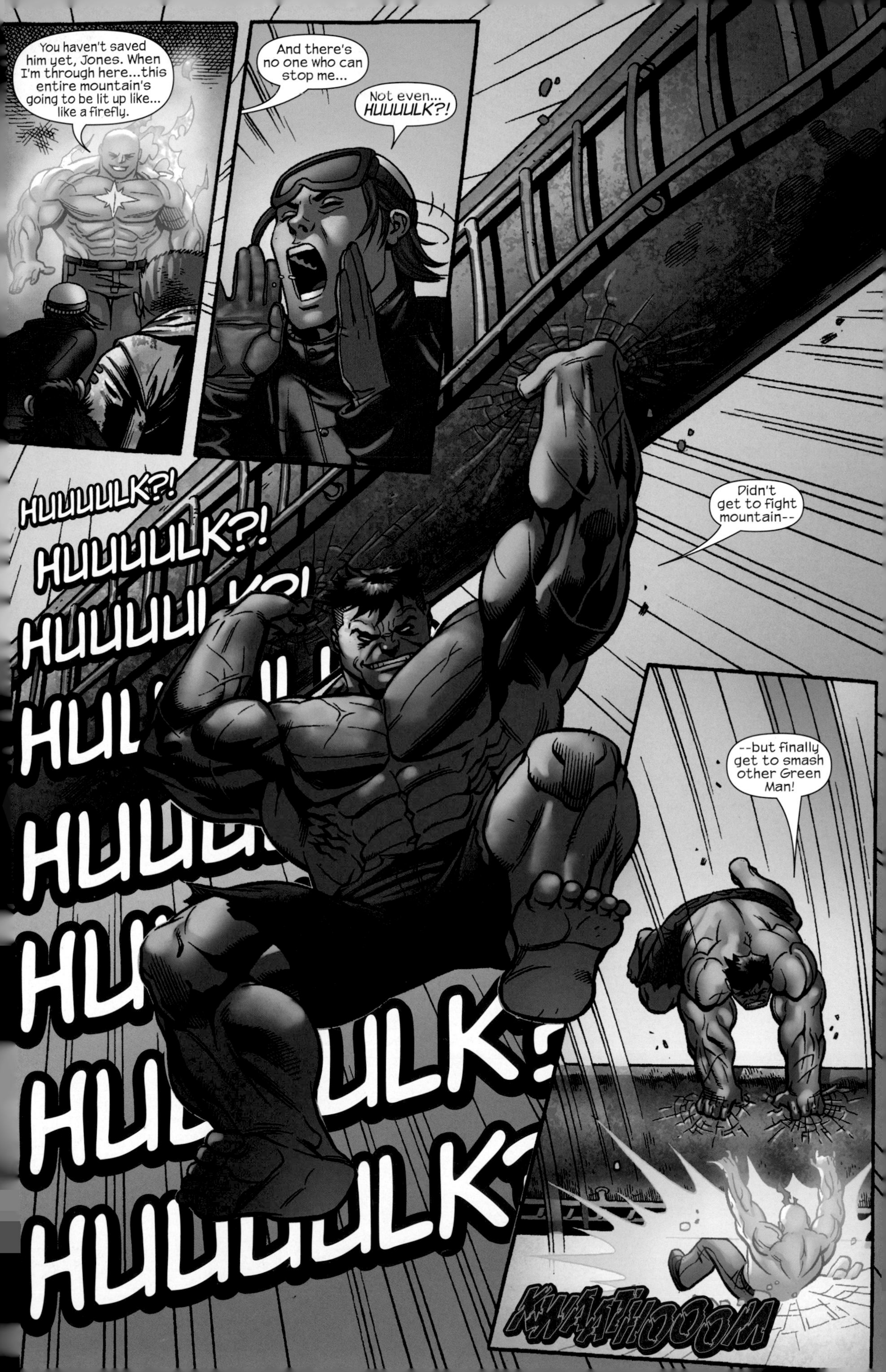
You haven't saved him yet, Jones. When I'm through here...this entire mountain's going to be lit up like... like a firefly.
And there's no one who can stop me...
Not even... HUUUULK?!
HUUUULK?!
HUUUULK?!
Didn't get to fight mountain--
--but finally get to smash other Green Man!
KWAATHOOOOM

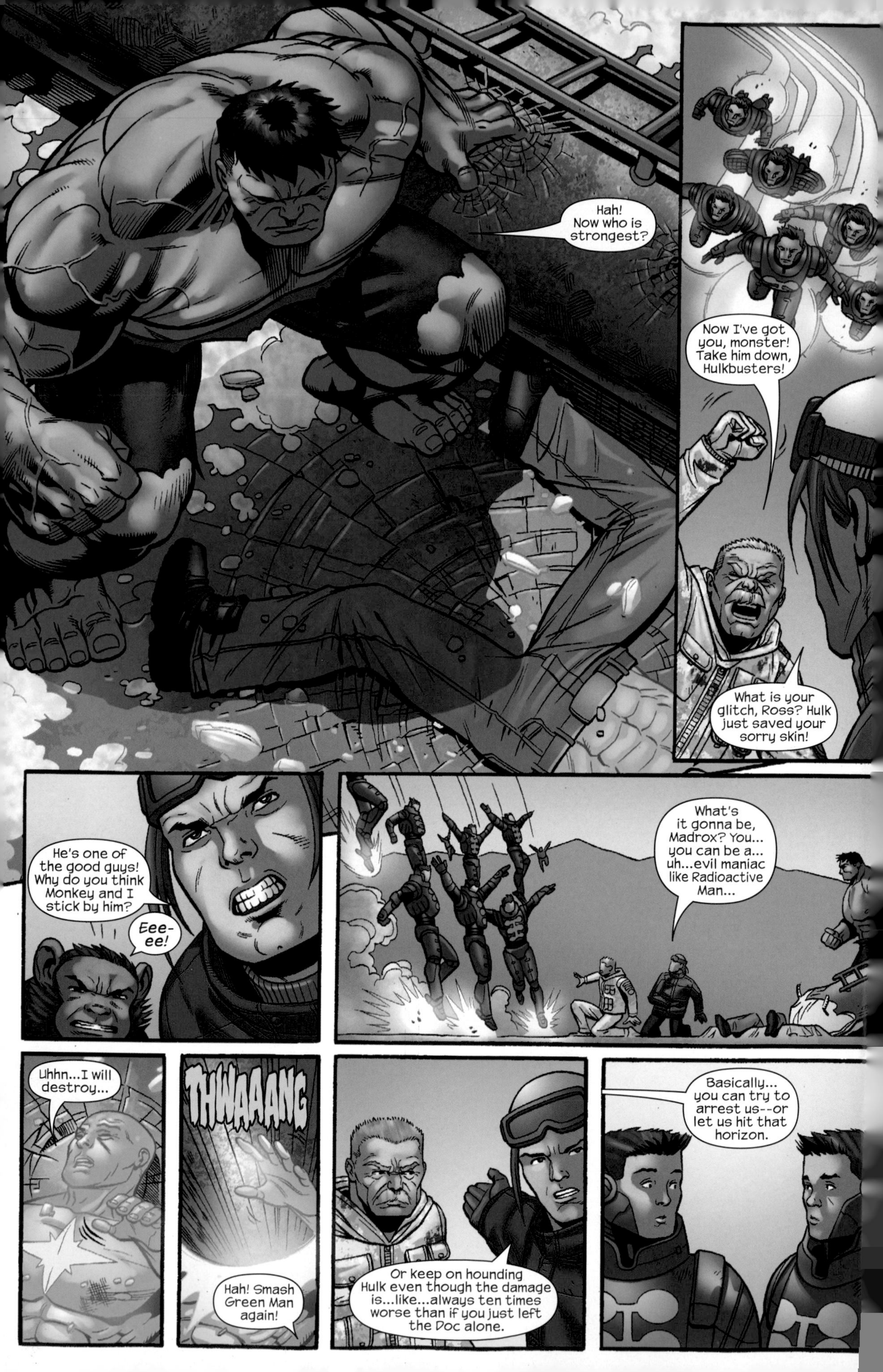
Hah! Now who is strongest?
Now I've got you, monster! Take him down, Hulkbusters!
What is your glitch, Ross? Hulk just saved your sorry skin!
He's one of the good guys! Why do you think Monkey and I stick by him?
Eee-ee!
What's it gonna be, Madrox? You... you can be a... uh...evil maniac like Radioactive Man...
Uhhn...I will destroy...
THWAAANG
Hah! Smash Green Man again!
Or keep on hounding Hulk even though the damage is...like...always ten times worse than if you just left the Doc alone.
Basically... you can try to arrest us--or let us hit that horizon.

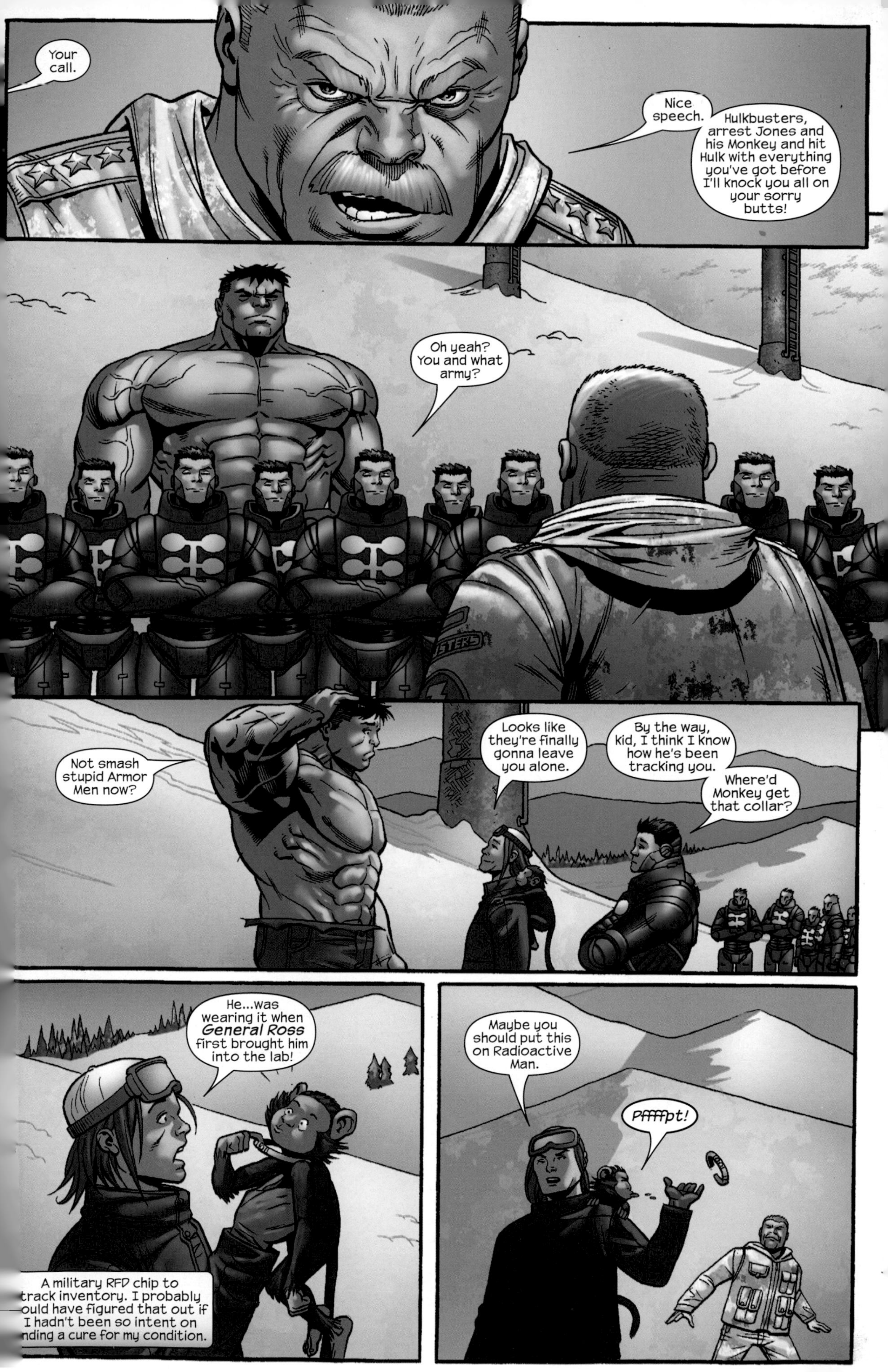
Your call.
Nice speech.
Hulkbusters, arrest Jones and his Monkey and hit Hulk with everything you've got before I'll knock you all on your sorry butts!
Oh yeah? You and what army?
Not smash stupid Armor Men now?
Looks like they're finally gonna leave you alone.
By the way, kid, I think I know how he's been tracking you.
Where'd Monkey get that collar?
He...was wearing it when General Ross first brought him into the lab!
A military RFD chip to track inventory. I probably ould have figured that out if I hadn't been so intent on nding a cure for my condition.
Maybe you should put this on Radioactive Man.
Pfffffpt!

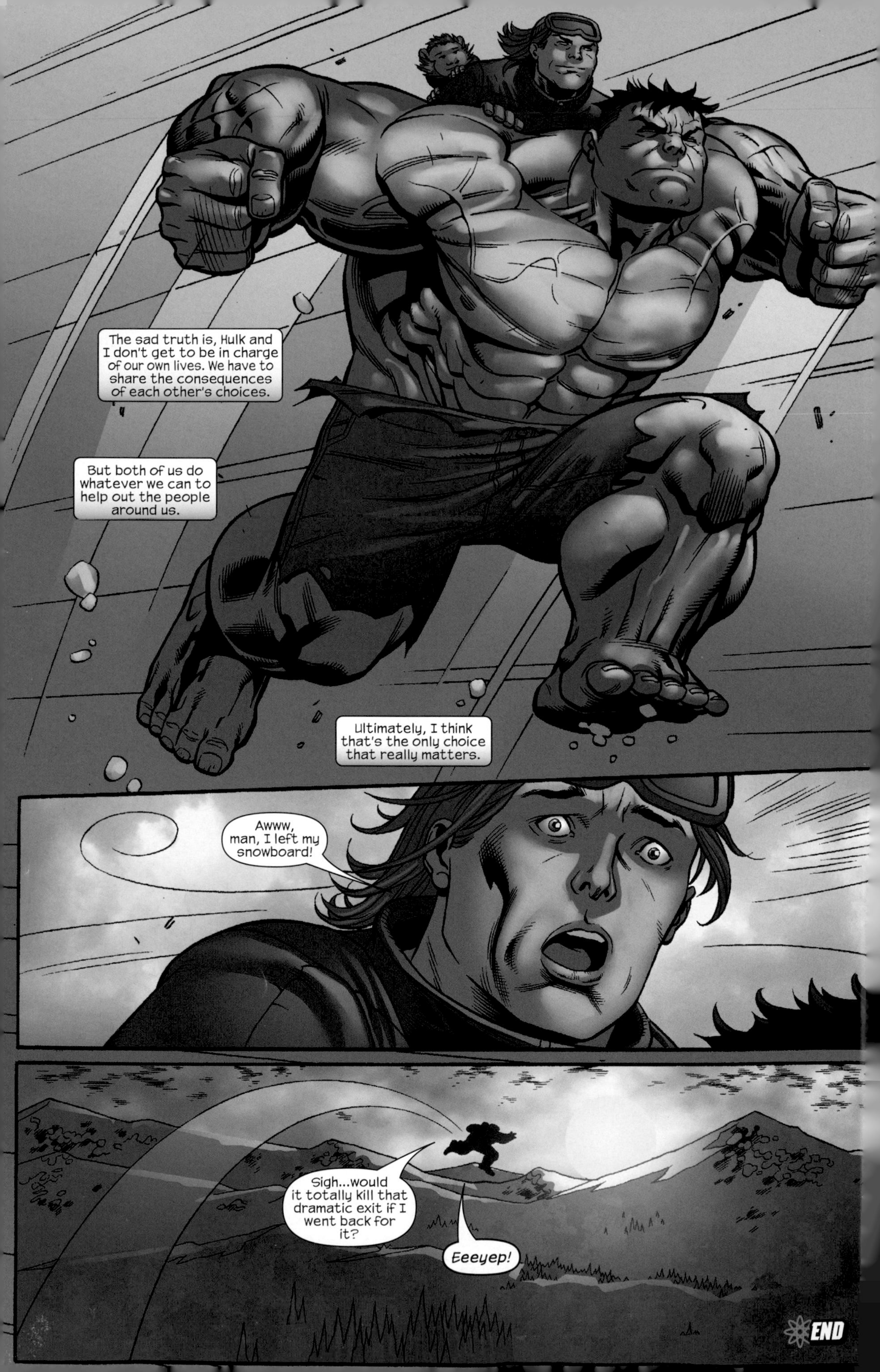
The sad truth is, Hulk and I don't get to be in charge of our own lives. We have to share the consequences of each other's choices.
But both of us do whatever we can to help out the people around us.
Ultimately, I think that's the only choice that really matters.
Awww, man, I left my snowboard!
Sigh...would it totally kill that dramatic exit if I went back for it?
Eeeyep!
END